GW00866152

Mike & The Magic Marble

WRITTEN BY
Stephen Kempain
ILLUSTRATED BY
Jordan Kempain

by MIKE

Mike was bored.

…and a little lonely.

There was no one around, and his Dad was in his office working. Mike loved his Dad but he always seemed too busy. He wished his dad would spend time with him and on their project.

BEST
DAD

So Mike went outside to the back yard. He tried shooting baskets, but couldn't seem to sink anything. He tried counting clouds, but it was a beautiful sunny and cloudless day. Then he set an empty soda can on an upside down pail and threw rocks at it, but try as he might, he couldn't knock it over. So he set up 3 cans and got a little closer. But no matter how hard he tried, he couldn't hit one. Now he was bored, lonely and getting frustrated as well.

He decided he didn't want to play that game anymore, so he lined up the cans on the grass to kick them across the yard. As he was winding up for a tremendous kick, something shiny moved in front of him. That's when Mike found the marble. He was puzzled because he didn't play with marbles...and he was sure the marble was moving when he first saw it. How did the marble get there?

RUCK
SODA

It was a little bigger than the marbles he'd seen before. It had shades of green with swirls of white. But most interesting of all, was that you could see into the glass where the swirls created patterns like on the planets Jupiter and Saturn. As he turned the marble in the sun different glints of color flickered inside and seemed to change with each different position. He had never seen a marble like this.

He rushed inside the house and into his Dad's office to show him the marble. "Look what I found" Mike proudly said to his Dad. "That's nice" was all his Dad could say. He didn't even look up but kept right on working. Mike was disappointed at his Dad's reaction and now he felt guilty for bothering him. Mike walked slowly away. He knew he shouldn't interrupt him, but the marble was so different. He was starting to feel sad again, but just then, he almost dropped the marble and juggled it from hand to hand. It was like the marble was moving on its own. He couldn't get a grip on it and finally trapped it against his chest.

BEST
DAD

He went into the living room thinking about what he could do with it. First he kneeled on a patch of floor where a sun beam shone. After staring at it in the sunlight he decided to spin it around on the floor like a top. As it spun it picked up speed and continued to spin until Mike stopped it by putting his finger on top of it. On the second spin it spun and stopped abruptly, like Mike had put his finger on it, but he hadn't. Next he set up a domino and tried to roll it down from several feet away. He hit it the first time, and the marble rolled back and stopped right in front of him. The same thing happened on the second try…then again…he hit it every time and each time from further away and each time the marble rolled right back and stopped right in front of him.

So he set up a series of dominoes and toy bowling pins from across the room, he took careful aim and rolled it at the lead domino. He hit it and watched as everything he set up was knocked down. At times the marble looked like a blur. The marble bounced from domino to bowling pin and didn't stop until everything set up was knocked over and once again, the marble rolled right back to him. That's when Mike became a little scared. Mike realized he was making noise. Noise his Dad wouldn't like, especially when he was working. But when he peaked around the corner, his Dad still had his head down, looking at a computer screen.

“Dad? Is the noise bothering you?” Mike asked.

His Dad poked his head out of his office. He had a puzzled look on his face as he asked, “What noise? Did you break something?”

“No” was all Mike could say as he turned to walk away.

He was upset. He hadn't broken anything, but he was puzzled too. He was making a lot of noise. He peaked again at his Dad, now working, and bounced the marble on the floor. It made no noise and came right into his hand!

He walked back into the living room and rolled the marble at the toy bowling pins that were set up in the corner of the room. Crash! It was a Strike! All of the pins were knocked over and the marble was in front of him again. Mike put the marble in his pocket and again peaked around the corner. Dad acted as though nothing had happened.

Mike was just getting ready to set the pins back up, when his Dad came into the room. Ah, thought Mike, he did hear the pins, but all he did was smile at Mike and look around the room. Then he went back into the office and moved some papers around, then back into the living room and then into the kitchen.

CRASH!

"What are you looking for?" Mike asked his Dad.
"I need to find my keys. We need to go the store after you clean up the living room" Dad said. They both looked around the room. All of the toys were put away. The dominoes were back in their box. Even the pins were back in their basket! Mike hadn't touched them. That's when Mike knew the marble was special, like magic. He was just about to get the marble out of his pocket when his Dad stood in front of him. "Well, I guess we can go as soon as I find my keys. I thought I left them right here" he said, pointing at the kitchen counter.

Just then the marble fell to the floor. Mike didn't know how it happened since it had been safely in his pocket. Mike chased after it, but it bounced on the floor and rolled away, just out of his grasp and disappeared under the couch. When he crawled to where it had rolled he spied something under the couch. "Daddy! Are those your keys?" Mike exclaimed as his Dad bent down to look. "Yes!" his Dad nearly shouted. "Thanks Mike!" "It was my marble." said Mike. "Marble?" his Dad asked. "I found it outside." Mike said as he handed the marble to his Dad.

"My, that's a beauty" his Dad said with some interest. "This marble is amazing!" Mike said. He started to tell his Dad all about the strange things the marble could do. Dad smiled and listened to Mike as Mike became more and more excited. Mike was about to show his Dad some if the things the marble could do when Dad interrupted. "Tell you what, Kiddo. Let's go into town and get some supplies I need for work and for dinner. When we get back, we can work on our project."

Mike was so happy he jumped into his Dad's arms! He loved to work on the project with his Dad. When they got outside Mike begged his Dad to try rolling the marble into a hole in the driveway. Mike got it in the hole every time. But when his Dad tried, he couldn't make it once. After many tries, they agreed to go to the store.

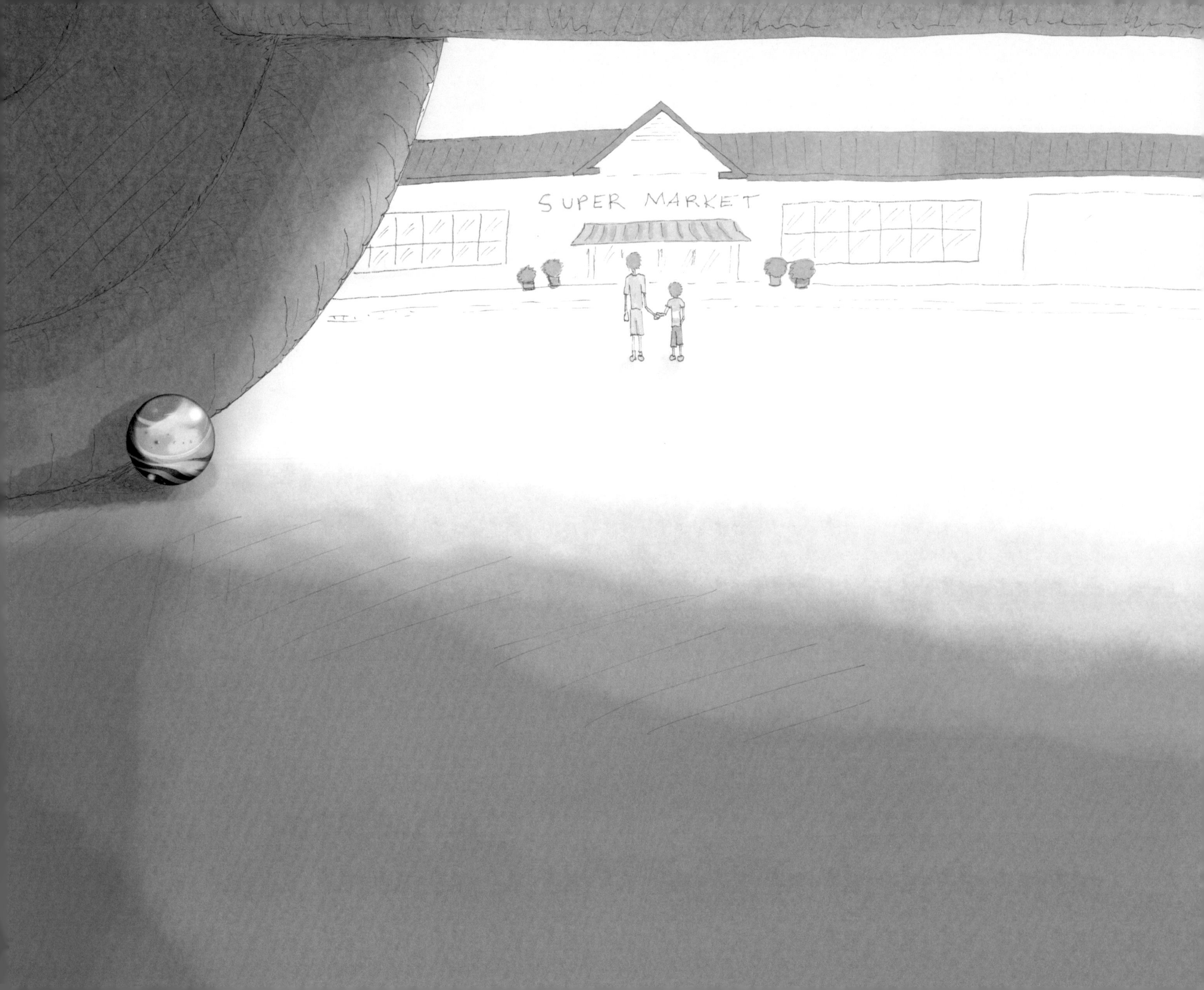
SUPER MARKET

As they got into the car Mike put the marble into his pocket and they drove out of the driveway and down the street. When they got to the store, Mike got out of the car seat. As he got out of the car he didn't notice it, but the marble slipped out of his pocket and rolled unnoticed under a car next to theirs.

Mike held his Dad's hand as they went into the store to shop for all of the things he needed. Mike even got a Popsicle! Once they got back into the car Mike reached into his pocket for the marble. "It's gone!" Mike frantically said. Mike's Dad could see how upset Mike was, so he picked him up and held him, then they looked all around for the marble, but it was not to be found. "I'm sorry Mike. Maybe it will turn up. Let's go home. You can help me with the rest of the floor boards on the tree house before dinner" his Dad said. After a pause, he added, "You can help with dinner too". Mike was very upset about the marble, but he was happy too. He wasn't lonely or bored anymore.

The marble saw the whole thing, and was glad.

So, it rolled out from under the car and
down the street…

Then it rolled up to a little girl who was
sitting on the sidewalk.

She was bored…
and a little lonely.

— THE END —

"To my dad, thank you
for always spending time with me
so I did not need a magic marble."

— JORDAN KEMPAIN

STEPHEN KEMPAIN (AUTHOR), JORDAN KEMPAIN (ILLUSTRATOR), & HOLLIS KEMPAIN 1990's

Lightning Source UK Ltd.
Milton Keynes UK
UKRC031109131022
410418UK00002B/23